Namaste, Ölyk.

Rynka Kriya

Namaste, Ölyk.
Copyright © 2021 by Rynka

Tellwell Talent
www.tellwell.ca

ISBN
978-0-2288-2237-0 (Paperback)
978-0-2288-5791-4 (ebook)

Acknowledgement

They say it takes a village to raise a child. Without my village of people who helped me through this entire journey, this would not have been possible. Special thanks from the bottom of my heart to those who helped me in making this book possible. To my amazing brother & editor, Thomas Grout, my very patient, publishing team-especially Rhea Mae Inot, all the Chrea family in Cambodia, the Grouts family, Auntie-Beth (Gienger), Janet and all of the Amsdens, the Radfords, my inspiration, Marni Turek, Anne Uebbing, Astro's second mom - Melissa Chaun, the Muraoka family, Obachama, Baaba, my children Nina, Kenzo & Astro and of course, my best friend/husband, Riti Chrea. And of course, a big, big thank you to you, who's holding this book now. I deeply hope this book finds you peace and joy with your loved ones. Namaste, to all.

In memory of Kenryu Bizenjima

DEAR Elliot,
Happy happy holidays!
Hope you enjoy this book!!
From, Rynka

Namaste, Ölyk.

The sun went down.

The moon is up.

The forest is asleep.

2

...But not this pup.

Ölyk, Ölyk,

4

...couldn't sleep.

Ölyk tried and tried  to find his peace.

First, he tried counting sheep.

 He practiced all his ABC's,

and even tried to
catch the Z's.

"He reread all of Socrates...

in Japanese."

Ölyk, Ölyk,

couldn't sleep.

So he decided,

before this warm night ends...

Two steps in,
two breath deep,
who did he see
up in a tree?

"Mrs. Snake, Mrs. Snake, play with me."

Mrs. Snake climbed down and said, "Ölyk, Ölyk, perhaps instead we'll find our peace and go to bed."

"This is how I find my peace.

Tummy down,
put your arms to your side,
now stretch out your neck.
Breathe in. Breathe out."

"Breathe in. Breathe out,"
repeated Ölyk.

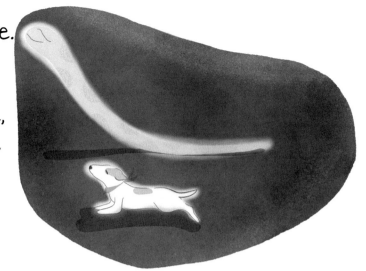

"Namaste, Mrs. Snake."
"Namaste, Ölyk."

Two steps more
and who does he spot
grooming a top
an old clay pot?

"Mr. Bobcat, Mr. Bobcat, play with me."

Mr. Bobcat stepped down and said,
"Ölyk, Ölyk, perhaps instead
we'll find our peace and go to bed."

"On all fours, drop your head,
now round your back
and find your belly
button.
Breathe in.
Breathe out."

"Breathe in. Breathe out."
"Namaste, Mr. Bobcat."

"Namaste, Ölyk."

A few steps more,
"then" a bit beyond,
who did he find in the pond?

15

"Brother Flamingo, Brother Flamingo,
play with me."

Brother Flamingo raised his head,
"Ölyk, Ölyk, perhaps instead
we'll find our peace and go to bed."

Stand on one leg
and hold the other foot.
Now reach for the sky
and smile to the moon.

Breathe in.
Breathe out."

"Breathe in.
Breathe out."

"Namaste, Brother Flamingo."
"Namaste, Ölyk."

Around a corner,
across a plank,
who did he see
on the river bank?

"Granny Turtle, Granny Turtle, play with me."

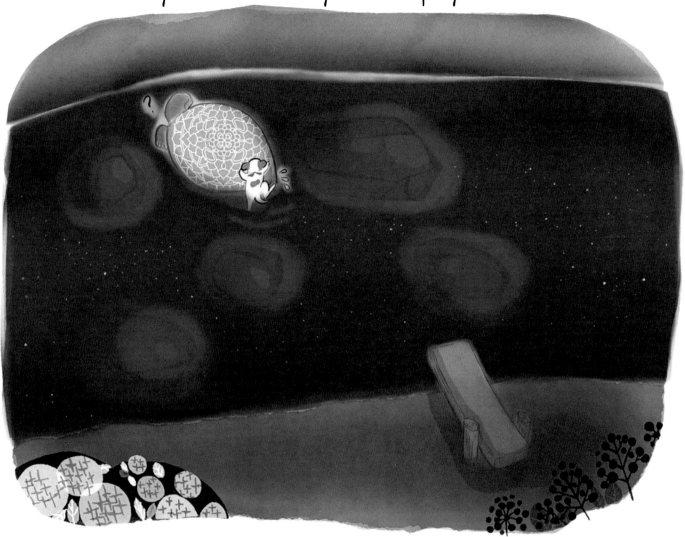

Granny Turtle slowly came out and said,
"Ölyk, Ölyk, perhaps instead
we'll find our peace and go to bed."

"Sit down on your hip, arms under your knees, now fold your body forward and extend your neck.

Breathe in. Breathe out."

"Breathe in. Breathe out."

"Namaste, Granny Turtle."
"Namaste, Ölyk."

Two steps on and Olyk yawned.

What did he hear was now near?

"Uncle Lion, Uncle Lion...YAWN......play with me."

"Ölyk, Ölyk, perhaps instead
we'll find our peace and go to bed."

Sit proud and tall.

Press your paws
down strong.

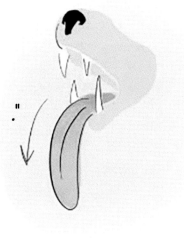

Breathe in. . .
Now stick your tongue out and. . ."

21

Roarn

Roa

23

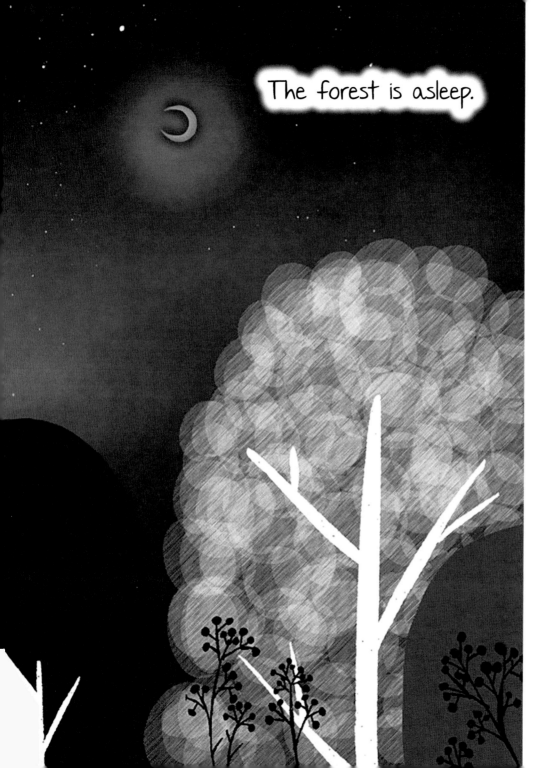

"Namaste, Ölyk."

Peace to all the children around the world.

ॐ a vi ra hūm kham vajra-dhātu vam.

How to play with Animal Yoga Cards

Flashcards
Go through the cards and try poses together with the players.

Who's Missing?
Line up 3-5 animal cards in front of you, face up. Go over all of them together. Tell players to close their eyes. Then flip one card face down while their eyes are closed. Let them open their eyes and ask, "Who's missing?" Players need to act out the pose as they answer.

Charades
After going over all of them, one player picks up one card and acts out the pose. Other players guess what animal pose it is. As they answer, they also have to act out the pose.

Reverse Charades
One player shows the card on top of the head without looking at the card. Then the whole group, except for that player, has to act out the card.

Matching Game
Make copies for each card. Lay them face down and find matches. As they find matches, players need to act out the poses.

Dice + Cards
Stack the cards and place them face down. Roll a die (or 2 to make larger number counts). Players need to hold the selected pose while breathing the number count of the die. (Breathing in-and-out is 1 count).

Bingo
On a scanner/copier, arrange the cards in a 3 x 3 grid pattern, leave a blank in the middle. Make a couple of different patterns. Players can take turns and cross off a grid while acting out the pose. For the middle blank square, they need to create an original animal pose to cross it off. Other players need to act out the pose together.

Jungle Scavenger Hunt
Hide the animal cards throughout in the room. Let the players find them. Each player needs to act out the pose on the card and let the others guess which animal they found.

CAT POSE
(BIDALASANA)

GIRAFFE POSE
(CHITROSSHTTRASANA)

TURTLE POSE
(KURMASANA)

COW POSE
(BITILASANA)

DOWNWARD DOG
(ADHO MUKHA SHVANASANA)

FLAMINGO   POSE
(MARICHY   ASANA)

35

BUTTERFLY POSE
(BADDHA KONASANA)

SNAKE POSE
(BHUJANGASANA)

LION POSE/BREATH
(SIMH ASANA)

CREATE YOUR OWN!

CREATE YOUR OWN!

CREATE YOUR OWN!

37

Rynka Kriya

An illustrator, yoga Instructor, animal & nature lover.
Resides near a beaver dam in Port Moody, BC, Canada.

Special thanks to my best furry son, Astro.

Manufactured by Amazon.ca
Bolton, ON

21650013R00029